Ballet Babes

Follow the Glitter Girls' latest adventures!
Collect the other fantastic books in the series:

Look out for the Glitter Girls summer special!

Sunshine Superstars

Caroline Plaisted

Ballet Babes

SCHOLASTIC

Scholastic Children's Books,
Commonwealth House, 1-19 New Oxford Street,
London WC1A 1NU, UK
a division of Scholastic Ltd

London ~ New York ~ Toronto ~ Sydney ~ Auckland
Mexico City ~ New Delhi ~ Hong Kong

Published by Scholastic Ltd, 2001

Copyright © Caroline Plaisted, 2001

ISBN 0 439 99404 7

Typeset by Falcon Oast Graphic Art Ltd
Printed and bound in Denmark by Nørhaven Paperback, Viborg

6 8 10 9 7

Chapter 1

Zoe looked out of her bedroom window and across her back garden. It was raining and it was cold. She would have begun to feel bored if she hadn't known that her best friends, Charly, Flo, Hannah and Meg, were going to arrive any minute. While she waited for them, Zoe looked around her bedroom. She'd decorated the walls with posters and pictures of horses, ponies and donkeys. Zoe loved animals and she wanted to be a vet when she was older.

Suddenly, there was a knock at the bedroom door.

RAT tat tat! It was the Glitter Girls' special knock!

"Who is it?" Zoe whispered.

"GG!" came the reply.

Immediately, Zoe opened her bedroom door. There stood Charly, Flo, Hannah and Meg. They were all smiling and ready to start the Glitter Girls' Sunday afternoon meeting!

★ ♥ ★ ♥ ★ ♥ ★

"Hi Zoe! I brought us these!" Meg said, walking in with a plate full of little cakes. Each of them was decorated with icing and covered with tiny sweets. They looked delicious!

"Hey, thanks!" Zoe said, taking the plate from her friend and putting it on her bedside table. "They look fab! Did you make them?"

"Yes – Sue helped me after lunch," explained Meg. Sue was Meg's older sister.

"And I brought this up as well," said Charly, holding up a jug full of juice.

"Here are the cups," said Hannah, as she put

down a collection of brightly coloured beakers next to the plate of cakes.

"I didn't bring anything with me . . . apart from this!" exclaimed Flo, taking off her bright pink mac and pulling a copy of the local paper out from underneath it. She shook off some rain, "Phew it's wet out there! So, have you lot seen this week's issue of the local paper?"

"No – why?" Meg asked, as she and the other Glitter Girls got comfy on the beanbags and cushions that were spread across Zoe's bedroom floor. Zoe had a great collection of them: some she'd made with the help of her older sisters. Others she'd either been given as presents or had saved up for and bought with her pocket money. Most of them were pink, but there were a few dark purple and mauve ones as well. And some had glittery thread shot through them and embroidery and jewels sewn into them. They were the perfect accessories for a Glitter Girl's bedroom!

"Well," said Flo dramatically, beginning to explain just why she'd brought the paper with her, "there's a story about the hospital radio in it."

"Really?" asked Charly, trying to grab the paper from Flo.

The Glitter Girls were always interested to hear more about the radio station. They'd once made a radio programme for the children in the hospital and occasionally they got asked back to help out.

"Come on Flo!" said Hannah, getting impatient. "Don't tease us! Tell us!"

"Yes, what does it say?" Zoe asked.

So Flo read the story to her friends:

" 'The hospital radio station is delighted to have taken delivery of a hundred new CDs. Thanks to the generosity of Media TV viewers, Cindy Curtis, presenter of Media Tonight, donated a spectacular selection of the latest tracks to the hospital on their behalf.' And there's a photo of Cindy giving the CDs to Suzy at the hospital."

"Cool!" said Charly, pushing her pink glasses back up her nose and grabbing the paper to look at it. "Isn't Cindy Curtis great?"

Each of the Glitter Girls looked at the story. They all had to agree with Charly. Cindy Curtis was really pretty and she always wore amazing clothes.

"We need another project like *Glitter FM*, don't we?" Meg asked her friends. "It was really good fun."

"Yes, wasn't it?" said Charly.

"Hey – cake anyone?" Zoe asked. She couldn't sit and look at Meg's delicious cakes any longer and handed them round to her friends.

Hannah was the last to look at the paper and, once she'd finished reading about the hospital radio, she started to flick through the other pages, glancing at the pictures and the headlines. Suddenly, her eyes caught a big advertisement.

"Hey – listen to this, girls! There's going to be a big talent competition at the Town Hall!"

"Let's have a look!" said Zoe, leaning over Hannah's shoulder.

"Cool – I wonder who will enter?" Charly said.

A smile spread across Meg's face. "We could!" she said.

The other girls looked at her for a second, then they all began smiling and giggling.

"Go Glitter!" they all shouted.

When they had all calmed down a little bit, Meg, practical as ever, asked, "So when is this competition and how old do you have to be to enter?"

"Oh, don't say we won't be able to join in the fun!" said Charly anxiously.

"Let me look at the rules," said Hannah, who still had the newspaper. She quickly read through the rules of entry that were printed next to the announcement for the competition.

"What does it say?" Zoe asked.

"Well," explained Hannah, "the competition is in four weeks' time and there are two sections to it. One's for people over sixteen and the other is for people below that age. That's us!"

Flo took her thumb out of her mouth. "Four weeks! That's not very long though, is it?"

"It would certainly be difficult for us to organize something for a talent competition in such a small amount of time," agreed Zoe.

"So, what are we going to do?" Charly asked. "Are we going to enter this competition or not?"

11

Chapter 2

"I think we should do it!" said Flo.

"Yes – it would be great fun!" agreed Zoe.

"But can we put something together that's good enough in only four weeks?" asked Meg.

"And what would we do?" Hannah wondered.

"Could we sing something?" Zoe asked. Like the rest of the Glitter Girls, Zoe sang in the school choir.

"I'm not sure," Meg said, munching a mouthful of cake. "I bet loads of people will sing, won't they? Hey, I know! Why don't we play some music? I'd love to play my cello!"

"Yes, but you're the only one who's really good at music, Meg," Flo mumbled, her mouth full of cake too. "The rest of us can only play the recorder."

"Flo's right," Hannah declared. "Maybe we should all enter separately? You know, doing the things we like best?"

The Glitter Girls thought about it for a moment or two. Meg could easily play her cello – she was really good at it. And Zoe and Flo could sing a duet. Charly, who wanted to be a television presenter, could read a poem or recite something from a play like she did at the last school concert. And Hannah, who wanted to be a ballet dancer, could perform a dance.

"There's just one problem," said Meg, looking at the others.

"What's that?" Hannah asked.

"It would be awful competing against each other, wouldn't it?" Meg replied. "I mean, what if one of us won the prize?"

"Well, it would be great for one of us, wouldn't it?" said Zoe. She was the youngest of three sisters and used to sharing things.

"But I'd hate it if I won on my own!" wailed Hannah. "Especially if you lot were taking part as well."

"So would I!" agreed Meg.

"Well, that's settled then," Charly declared. "Isn't it?"

"Yes," said Meg, determined as ever. "We'll just have to enter together, won't we?"

"And we've got to make sure we do it this week," Hannah said. "The competition closes to new entries next Friday!"

★　♥　★　♥　★　♥　★

Half an hour later, the Glitter Girls were still in deep discussion about what they should do.

"I know!" said Hannah. She was twiddling her long ginger hair around her fingers like she always did when she was thinking. "We could play some music, with Meg on the cello and the rest of us playing our recorders, couldn't we?"

"I'm not sure about that," said Zoe. "It's just that I'm so bad at the recorder that I'd let the rest of you down. The only thing I'm any good at is riding ponies – and I don't think they'd let me bring a pony into the Town Hall, would they."

Hannah and the others laughed.

"We could do a play!" Flo suggested. "Then each of us would have the chance to be a different character."

"And we could dress up, too!" said Hannah, who loved the idea of wearing a costume.

"It's an idea," agreed Meg, "but I'm not sure we'd have time to do a whole play."

"That's true," said Charly. "Hey, Hannah, is there a time limit for how long we're allowed to be on the stage?"

Hannah quickly looked at the rules in the paper. "Umm. . . Oh, here it is!" She quickly read it to herself and then said, "It says a maximum of ten minutes."

"It would be hard to fit a play into ten minutes," said Meg.

"Yes," Flo agreed. "Especially one that's got any kind of story to it."

"So, what is there that we all do, apart from going to swimming lessons and going to school?" Zoe asked, feeling exasperated.

"It's obvious!" said Charly. "We all do ballet, don't we? We could do a ballet!"

It was true. Every week, the Glitter Girls went to the local ballet studio after school and did a ballet class together with some other girls from local schools. Hannah also had an extra lesson on her own each week, as she was the best dancer of them all. So when Charly suggested it, they all agreed at once.

"It's a perfect idea!" said Meg. "We need a story to work around though."

"And some music!" said Zoe.

"And costumes," Flo added.

"And scenery and stuff!" Hannah finished.

"There's a lot to do, isn't there?" said Zoe.

"We can do it!" Meg declared, determined to make it happen. "First of all, we've got to decide what ballet we're going to do. Then we can work out which of us is going to do each job."

"Hmm. . ." said Hannah. "A traditional ballet might take a *lot* of work. Maybe we could do a modern dance instead."

The Glitter Girls had just started to do modern dance at the ballet studio. You could do it without ballet shoes on and have fun dancing to music more like pop music than traditional ballet music. She knew that Charly and Zoe already preferred modern dance to ballet.

"Good idea!" said Flo.

"Yes – I like it!" agreed Zoe.

It looked like it was settled!

"OK," said Meg. "We need to write a list!"

The others laughed and Zoe quickly grabbed some paper and a pen from her desk and handed them to her friend. "Here," she said. "Well, I think that Hannah should work out the steps and things because she's best at dancing."

Everyone agreed.

"What about the music?" asked Zoe. "Meg, can you sort that out?"

"Sure," Meg nodded.

"And I'm sure my mum will help us out with the costumes," said Hannah.

"We could all help with the sewing, couldn't we?" said Charly.

"We'll need some scenery as well," said Hannah. "Do you think you could organize that Flo? You're brilliant at art!"

"Sure!" she said. "And I can probably get Kim to help out as well." Kim was Flo's older sister and she was even better at art than Flo!

"So, that's sorted then," Meg drew a line under her list. "Now all we've got to do is fill in this entry form and make sure we hand it in at the Town Hall before Friday!"

"Go Glitter!" they all said.

Another Glitter Girl adventure had begun!

 # Chapter 3

Charly's mum met the Glitter Girls after school on Monday afternoon. First they went to the Town Hall so that the girls could hand in their entry form for the talent competition. Then they went to the library to look at some books about modern dance to give them some ideas about costumes and scenery.

"Is it OK if I meet you back here in about half an hour?" asked Charly's mum. "Lily and I need to get some shopping for tea." Lily was Charly's younger sister and a Glitter Girl in the making.

"Terrific!" the girls all said at once. "See you later, Mrs Fisher. Bye Lily!"

"Go Glitter!" Lily called, waving her arms in the air just like she had seen the Glitter Girls do.

★ ♥ ★ ♥ ★ ♥ ★

Once they were in the library, the Glitter Girls had a great time going through all the dance books they could find.

"Hey, look at that!" said Flo, pointing to a picture of two dancers. The female dancer was being held upside down in the air by the man she was dancing with. "How do they do that?"

"Isn't it amazing?" agreed Charly.

"I'd just love to be good enough to do that!" said Hannah. "But come on, let's see if there are any other books we can use."

Flo managed to find a book about scenery that would be just perfect for helping her to create the backdrop for their dance. Charly found one all about stage make-up.

"Hey, that looks great!" said Meg.

"How are you getting on with the music?" Hannah asked. "Did you have time to find some last night?"

"Well, I had a word with my mum about it," said Meg, "and she suggested some music called 'Popcorn'. She said it sounds like lots of popcorn popping all over the place."

"Hey, didn't Mrs McArthur play that once in one of our classes?" Charly asked. Mrs McArthur was the girls' ballet teacher.

"Yes, she did!" said Flo, starting to hum the tune.

"Shh!" hissed Meg. "We're in the library, don't forget!"

The Glitter Girls giggled and looked around. Fortunately, the library was quite empty and anyway, no one seemed to have heard them.

"I recognize that music!" whispered Hannah. "I think it sounds great! I reckon we could do something terrific to that!"

"Well, we'll have to discuss it tomorrow," said Zoe, looking at her watch, "Come on – we've got to meet your mum!"

★　♥　★　♥　★　♥　★

In the lunch queue the next day, the Glitter Girls were busy chattering away about the competition when one of the girls in the group in front of them suddenly said, "Oh, have you entered the talent show as well?"

"Yes, we have," Meg replied. "Isn't it exciting! What are you doing in the competition?"

"We're doing a modern dance that we've choreographed ourselves," the girl explained. "How about you?"

The Glitter Girls were dumbstruck! They were doing a modern dance too? They couldn't!

For a moment or two, none of them could think of what to say. Eventually, Hannah mumbled, "Oh, we're doing a dance too – but we're not sure of the style just yet. . ."

"Sounds great!" said the girl, smiling. "We'll be competing against each other then!"

The Glitter Girls couldn't believe how calm

the other girls were at finding out about them all being in the same competition.

"Yes, I s'pose so," Meg replied, her voice squeaking a bit in panic.

The Glitter Girls carried on queuing in complete silence. It wasn't until they sat down at one of the tables to actually eat their lunch that they spoke about the bombshell that had just been dropped.

"So they're going to do a modern dance too?" Hannah sounded as worried as she looked.

"Yep," said Charly. "They go to that other ballet school at the church hall, don't they?"

"I bet they're really good, too," Hannah sighed.

"Well it doesn't matter if they are, does it?" said Meg. The other Glitter Girls looked at her.

"If they're better than us, then we won't do very well, will we?" Zoe replied.

"But it's a competition, isn't it?" said Charly.

"I mean, we knew when we entered that there would be other people showing off their talents as well, didn't we?"

"Yes, Charly's right," said Meg. "Course we want to do our best. But if we lose – well, we'll just have to try again next year, won't we?"

"You don't get it though, do you?" Hannah tried to explain as she pushed her lunch around on her plate. "We can't *both* do a modern dance. I mean, that's why I didn't tell her that we were going to do a modern dance as well. We can't have two groups of girls doing pretty much the same thing, can we?"

She looked around at the other Glitter Girls.

Suddenly they understood what Hannah meant.

"We've got to think of something else we can do!" exclaimed Meg.

Chapter 4

"It's a disaster!" said Hannah, picking at her food.

"But we can do something about it, can't we?" said Flo.

"Like what?" Hannah asked.

"Like do one of the other ideas we thought of," suggested Charly.

"But the only thing we all agreed that we could all do well was dance!" said Hannah.

"She's right," sighed Flo, sucking her thumb in thought.

Charly pushed her glasses back up her nose and said, "So what are we going to do then?"

"I'm not sure," said Meg, thinking.

"Well, Hannah just said that the only thing we

can all do well is dance, didn't she?" Zoe looked around at her friends.

"Well, yes," agreed Charly.

"So, let's dance then!" said Zoe.

"Zoe, have you been listening at all?" Hannah was feeling very depressed about the competition and it showed.

"Course I have, duh-brain!" Zoe said. "But we don't have to do a modern dance – we could do a ballet, couldn't we?" Zoe explained.

"A ballet?" Hannah was starting to think along the same lines as Zoe. "What, like a classical ballet – one with a story?"

"That's a brilliant idea!" said Charly.

"Let's do it!" Flo agreed.

"But which story?" Meg wondered.

"I went to see *Sleeping Beauty* at the theatre once with my gran. It was gorgeous – all the dancers wore beautiful tutus," said Charly.

"We can't do that one," explained Hannah, though she sounded a bit more cheerful. "The story is too long to reduce down to under ten minutes."

"I suppose you're right," Charly muttered, still dreaming of all the floaty costumes she'd so admired.

"What about *Swan Lake?*" Flo asked. "I saw that on the telly once."

"Same problem," said Hannah.

"I've got a video of *The Nutcracker* at home," said Zoe. "Would that be any good?"

"Yeah, that's got loads in it!" said Charly. "I remember we all watched it together last Christmas. Do you think that would be too complicated as well, Hannah?"

A grin was beginning to appear on Hannah's face. "Well, the whole story put together would be too long, yes."

"Come on, Hannah," said Zoe. "Tell us! We can see you've thought of something!"

"Well, I was just thinking," Hannah explained. "Yes, the whole story together would be too long. But we could take one bit of the story, couldn't we?"

"What, like the bit at the party in the beginning? When the girl . . . Clara I think she was called . . . yes, when Clara is given the Nutcracker doll by that magician!" said Meg, getting excited along with Hannah.

"Actually, I was thinking more of the bit when the Sugar Plum Fairy does her dance, surrounded by the other ballerinas that dance with her," said Hannah.

"Oh, you mean those ones like snowflakes?" asked Zoe.

"Hey, that would be cool!" said Flo.

"Yes, let's do it!" begged Charly.

"Do you think we can?" Hannah wondered aloud to her friends.

"Course we can!" said Meg, pleased that Hannah had cheered up.

"Go Glitter!" they all said.

★ ♥ ★ ♥ ★ ♥ ★

On Wednesday afternoon, Charly, Zoe, Hannah, Meg and Flo met up at Charly's house.

They raced upstairs, kicked off their shoes and were soon sitting sprawled across the floor of Charly's room. Like Zoe, Charly loved animals and she too had animals posted on the walls of her bedroom. And there were also some photographs of Gilbert, her guinea pig, and Rosy, her rabbit – they were so cute! All of the Glitter Girls loved them.

"So what do you think of this?" Charly asked, grabbing something from a hook behind her bedroom door. She stood in front of her friends and held up a dressing gown. It was made of the most gorgeous fleecy material and had silver embroidery running all around the edges of the deep pink fabric.

"It's gorgeous!" said Zoe.

"Where did you get it?" asked Flo.

"My godmother brought it the last time she came to visit," Charly explained. "She found it while she was on holiday in Italy. I just love it!" Charly hugged the soft material to her face.

"Oh, I wish I had one like it!" Meg said.

"Me too!" Hannah sighed.

All the Glitter Girls loved clothes and as often as they could they went shopping in search of anything pink and glittery!

"Come on, you lot!" said Meg. "We've got lots to organize."

Charly put the dressing gown back on the hook and Meg took out the list she had written the other day at Zoe's house.

"So, Hannah," Meg asked, "are you happy with the ballet?"

"I think so," she explained. "I've been think-ing about the music and stuff. And I've got some ideas for some steps. But I wondered if I could borrow your video of the ballet, Zoe? Then I could make sure I've got it right."

"No problem," Zoe replied. "I could get it for you this evening, if you like."

"Thanks!" said Hannah.

"Great!" said Meg. "Right, what other things have we got to sort out? Are you OK about the scenery Flo?"

"I think so," Flo explained, "but I need to see the ballet too, to work out what should be painted on it."

"Sounds to me like we all need to watch the video – for inspiration!" said Charly.

"Yes! Let's do that on Friday after school!" suggested Zoe. "Do you think you could all come for a sleepover? Then we could make a party out of it!"

"Yes!" they all agreed.

"We'll have to check it's OK with our parents, but I'm sure it won't be a problem, will it? It's never been one before!" said Meg.

The others agreed with her.

"Now," said Meg, looking at her list again.

"I can get a CD of the music from my dad." She ticked that job off her list.

"Where are we going to practise?" Charly asked.

"We need somewhere with enough space for us all to dance around." Hannah said.

"Do you think Mrs McArthur will let us use her studio?" Meg asked.

"She uses it every day," said Hannah. "It would never be free at the times we'd need it."

"No . . . you're right," Meg put the end of her pencil in her mouth and chewed it thoughtfully.

On the other side of the bedroom, Flo was sucking her thumb, thinking.

"Well, I've just asked my dad if we can paint the scenery in our garage. It's a big space," she said, talking through her thumb, "but it will be full of paint and stuff."

"Why didn't I think of that?" Zoe said.

"Think of what?" Charly asked.

"We could use *our* garage! I'm sure my mum

and dad wouldn't mind!" Zoe looked pleased with herself.

"And I've spoken to my mum about the costumes," said Hannah. "Mum said she would help us, but only if we do some of the sewing as well!"

"Sorted then!" Meg said, writing everything down in her notebook.

The thinking part of the Glitter Girls' meeting was over!

Chapter 5

On Friday afternoon, the girls met up in Zoe's garage to organize their rehearsals and get ready for their *Nutcracker* sleepover!

"Look," said Zoe. "I've fixed up my CD player in here, so that we can listen to the music."

"Great," said Hannah. She looked around the garage. "Let's pretend that the garage door is the front of the stage."

"So this is where the scenery goes then?" Flo asked. She was working out how many pieces of scenery they'd be able to have.

"That's right," Hannah smiled.

"Hey, here's the CD," said Meg, fishing it out of the pocket of her special Glitter Girl jacket. It was denim and had the letters GG specially embroidered in pink and silver on the back.

"Thanks!" said Hannah. "Can you put it on? It'll get us in the right mood!"

As they listened to the music, Charly, Zoe, Hannah, Meg and Flo cleared everything to the sides of the garage so that they had as much room as possible to dance. When they were finished, they stood back and admired their rehearsal studio.

"Shall we get changed now?" Charly asked. Like the other girls, she'd brought her pink ballet bag with her and was desperate to get started.

The girls all looked at Hannah to see what she thought.

"I'd love to," said Hannah, "but I don't really know exactly what the steps should be until we watch the video tonight."

"Can't we just do a practice class instead?" Flo pleaded.

"Yes – that would be great!" the others agreed.

"Go on Hannah! You could take it and pretend that you're Mrs McArthur!" suggested Charly.

"OK!" said Hannah. "Tell you what – let's move these deckchairs over and we can use the backs of them as pretend barres."

The others quickly lined the chairs up, changed into their leotards, and then Meg set *The Nutcracker* to play.

"Right, girls!" said Hannah, sounding exactly like Mrs McArthur. "In your positions please, and *pliés*. Are you ready? And one and two and three and—"

And the class began!

★ ♥ ★ ♥ ★ ♥ ★

Half an hour later, the Glitter Girls were just doing their *reverence* when Dr Baker, Zoe's mum, appeared in the garage. As the music was switched off, Dr Baker broke into applause.

"My, don't you look good!" she exclaimed.

"Hi Mum!" said Zoe, rushing over to give her mum a kiss. Dr Baker worked at the local hospital and had just arrived home from work.

"Hello darling, how are you?" Dr Baker smiled at her youngest daughter and her best friends. "I can see that you've all been very busy."

"Yes," said Hannah. "Thanks for letting us use your garage, Dr Baker."

"Oh, that's not a problem," replied Zoe's mum. "You know I'm always happy to help the Glitter Girls! Now I thought you might all like some tea – are you hungry?"

"Go Glitter!" they called out.

★ ♥ ★ ♥ ★ ♥ ★

After tea, the Glitter Girls changed out of their leotards and put on some of their favourite nightclothes.

Zoe's dad had kindly plugged in the Televideo machine in Zoe's bedroom so that the Glitter Girls could watch *The Nutcracker*. And Zoe's mum had made a delicious feast for the girls to nibble on while they watched.

"This is going to be *such* fun!" said Flo.

"I love Glitter Girl sleepovers!" agreed Meg.

"Can we start?" Charly wanted to know.

"Sounds good to me!" said Hannah.

"I'll put the video in then," Zoe replied.

And very soon, the Glitter Girls found themselves swaying to the overture music. . .

★ ♥ ★ ♥ ★ ♥ ★

"I loved the bit when the Sugar Plum Fairy twirled around between all of the Snowflakes, didn't you?" Flo sighed afterwards.

"The whole thing was just great!" said Meg, munching on the last piece of orange.

"Isn't it exciting when the Rat King dies!" Charly exclaimed.

"Yes – but the bit when Clara dances with the Prince is just awesome!"

The Glitter Girls watched as Hannah started to dance around them, imitating the steps that they had just watched on the video.

"Oh, Hannah, that's just great!" Meg said.

"Do you think we can all do it?" Hannah asked her friends.

"We've got the music, haven't we?" said Meg.

"And now we've all seen the ballet as well!" agreed Flo.

"We'll have Hannah's tip top steps!" Zoe exclaimed.

"And fantastic scenery from Flo," Charly added.

"And my mum's costumes – I'm sure they'll be amazing!" Hannah said.

The Glitter Girls looked around at each other. They were all feeling pleased and excited. Suddenly, none of them could resist, "Go Glitter!" they all yelled.

Chapter 6

It was a great sleepover. There was a lot of dancing and a great deal of fun and planning. But not much sleep! Zoe's mum came in twice to tell the girls that it was well after midnight *so please could they go to sleep!* but they were so excited about the dance of the Sugar Plum Fairy that they found it hard not to keep talking about it. Eventually though, they did fall asleep.

And on Saturday morning, the Glitter Girls were fast asleep when Dr Baker came in to wish them good morning.

Flo was the first one to stir from her sleeping bag – mostly because it was right by the bedroom door and she was closest to Zoe's mum.

She stretched her arms and rubbed the sleep out of her eyes.

"What time is it?" she croaked, her throat sore from all the talking and giggling the night before.

"Well past nine o'clock!" Dr Baker said.

From her bed, Zoe stretched and yawned. "Hi Mum," she muttered.

"So, you had a good time last night I think!" laughed Dr Baker as she watched the three other Glitter Girls beginning to stir from their slumber.

"It was g—" Hannah yawned, and then finished what she had started to say, "great!"

"Sorry if we kept you awake, Dr Baker," Meg said, sitting up in her sleeping bag.

"Yes, sorry," added Charly.

"Well," Dr Baker stepped over the Glitter Girls and made her way to the window, where she drew back the curtains. They were pink and covered with cartoon pictures of ponies. "I think if you all hurry up and get dressed, there might be some breakfast downstairs for you all in about fifteen minutes. Do you think you can manage that?"

"Yes!" they all replied. They may have had a feast last night but this morning the Glitter Girls were starving!

★　♥　★　♥　★　♥　★

After wolfing down their breakfast, Charly, Zoe, Hannah, Meg and Flo had only an hour left before they all had to go their separate ways. It was the weekend and they all had things that they wanted to do with their families.

"Let's just go into the garage and talk about stuff," suggested Zoe, after they had helped to clear away their dirty crockery.

"OK," Meg agreed, and the Glitter Girls set off down the hall and entered the garage from the door that linked the hall to the garage from the house.

"I thought we could have some scenery that looks like clouds," suggested Flo, "then the Sugar Plum Fairy can look as if she's dancing on the clouds with her snowflakes."

"Hey, that's a great idea!" said Meg.

"Will you do stuff for the sides of the stage as well?" asked Charly.

"I'm not sure," Flo replied. "I mean, we don't want it too crowded on the stage, do we?"

"That's true," Charly agreed. "And anyway, if there's too much to carry it will take too long for us to get everything on the stage before we even start to dance."

"I had a word with my dad and he said that he would ask your dads if they wouldn't mind helping us carry the scenery up on to the stage and with getting it to the Town Hall as well," said Flo.

"Brilliant!" said Meg, writing that down in her new sparkly pink notebook.

"Dad and I are going to go along to the Town

Hall later today and see if we can measure up the stage," added Flo.

As they were speaking, Hannah was already beginning to rehearse some steps to herself.

"Shall I put some music on?" Zoe asked.

Hannah looked at her watch. The Glitter Girls still had forty-five minutes before they all had to leave.

"Go on then! Let's dance!" Hannah grinned.

The Glitter Girls all slipped their ballet shoes on and got into position behind Hannah.

"Right, I thought we could all start by standing at the back of the stage like this," Hannah placed her feet in fifth position with her arms *en courant* and the others did so as well. "Then, as the music begins we *relévé* and run forward to the front of the stage. . ." Hannah did this as she spoke and the others followed behind her. "Then we stop, *chassée*, and finish with our arms *en courant*, right foot pointed behind and our bodies *en diagonale*."

Hannah turned and looked at her friends. "Shall we try it with the music?"

"Go Glitter!" they all replied.

The first proper rehearsal had begun!

★ ♥ ★ ♥ ★ ♥ ★

On Monday, Meg asked Flo how she and her dad had got on with their plans for the scenery.

"Oh, the lady at the Town Hall was really sweet," Flo explained. "She let us get right up on stage and take some measurements, so I think we know what we should be doing."

"I've been thinking," said Hannah. "You know, about taking a bit from *The Nutcracker*. I mean, do you think the audience will be able to understand what we are up to if they don't know which bit of the ballet we are doing?"

"Hannah's got a point," Zoe said. "Do you think we need to explain what's going on?"

"I think we do!" said Hannah.

"Yes, good idea," Meg jotted it down in her notebook. "And I think we all know who is the perfect person for writing a short piece about what our ballet is about and presenting it to the audience at the Town Hall."

"Charly!" said Hannah, Zoe and Flo.

"Me!" agreed Charly and grinned at all of her best friends. "I can easily sort that out!" she said, bubbling with excitement about the special role she was going to play in the ballet.

"So, are we still meeting at Zoe's after school for another rehearsal?" Meg asked.

"Hope so," said Hannah, "because my mum's going to come round and help us design the costumes tonight!"

Chapter 7

The Glitter Girls had already started rehearsing when Hannah's mum arrived.

"Hi girls!"

Meg zoomed over to the CD player to stop the music.

"Hello Mrs Giles!"

"Hi Mum!" said Hannah, giving her mum a kiss.

"You've certainly been very busy over the last week!" said Hannah's mum. "I can't wait to see the ballet. Now, are you ready for me to measure you all up? Then we can have a chat about the costumes."

"Who do you want to do first?" Meg asked.

"Well, why don't I start with you?" Mrs Giles

suggested. She took a notebook and tape measure out of her work basket. "Arms up!" she told Meg.

Mrs Giles scribbled down some numbers. "Now your waist," she said, jotting things down again. "And one final measurement. . ." She measured the distance between Meg's waist and her knees. "Right, that's you done. Now, who's next?"

When all the Glitter Girls had been measured, Mrs Giles got a large sketchpad out of her work basket and said, "I've been thinking about the costumes you girls are going to need and I wondered if these were the sort of things you had in mind?"

Hannah's mum opened up the sketchbook and revealed drawings showing five girls – who all looked remarkably similar to each of the five Glitter Girls – wearing gossamer tutus. One of the sketches was labelled "Sugar Plum Fairy" and showed Hannah in a tutu of plum-coloured pink. A wisp of silky chiffon fabric had been attached to the frilly skirt and some sequins had been attached to the bodice. The other four pictures were labelled "Snowflakes" and showed Charly, Zoe, Flo and Meg in shimmering white tutus with slightly longer skirts. Their bodices had a swatch of silvery-white stretch fabric attached to them which glistened in the light. According to the sketch, their tutu skirts would have large silvery-white sequins glued to them and a border of tiny pearl-like sequins hanging from the hems.

As soon as the Glitter Girls saw them, they each had butterflies in their tummies and stood with their mouths open not knowing what to say.

"Don't you like them, girls?" Hannah's mum asked, sounding worried.

"They're just . . . just . . . just . . . amazing!" Meg finally managed to say on behalf of all of them.

"So you do like them then?" Hannah's mum laughed.

"Like them?" Flo said. "It looks as though they're going to be gorgeous!"

"They're perfect!" Charly spluttered.

"Brilliant!" added Zoe, gently touching the fabric swatches with her fingers.

"Oh thanks, Mum!" Hannah cried, giving her mum a huge hug.

"Well, I'm glad you like them! Now, it's going to be quite tough managing to make this lot in only three weeks," explained Mrs Giles. "Charly's mum has kindly said that she will help me to make up the basic costumes. But I am going to need your help to decorate them all with the sequins and things. I thought you could each add those to your own costumes while I make up the headdresses for you. I thought you could wear something like these. . ."

Mrs Giles showed the Glitter Girls another sketch, this time five separate portraits from the neck up showing the girls wearing tiny crowns. Hannah's had little tiny plums hanging down. "I'm going to make those out of tiny glass beads," Hannah's mum explained. The others had silver snowflakes dangling from them. "Hopefully they'll look just like snow falling as you dance," Mrs Giles said.

"My costume looks just like it's got sugar shimmering all over it!" exclaimed Hannah.

"And the snowflakes are going to look as if we are falling down from the sky!" said Flo enthusiastically.

"That's the general idea," said Hannah's mum, pleased that the girls liked her ideas. "So are you going to be able to help me make them, girls?"

"Go glitter!" they all agreed!

★ ♥ ★ ♥ ★ ♥ ★

Zoe, Hannah, Charly, Meg and Flo spent the next couple of weeks practising for the competition whenever they could. Almost every night, they met up in Zoe's garage to rehearse, until they were absolutely perfect. They even knew the music off by heart and went around humming the tune to themselves!

With two weeks to go before the competition, Hannah's and Charly's mums brought the costumes round to Zoe's garage on the Saturday morning for the Glitter Girls to try on. They had been rehearsing already that morning, and it didn't take them long to get out of their leotards and slip on their tutus.

"Well, don't you look wonderful!" exclaimed Charly's mum.

The Glitter Girls certainly felt fantastic in the costumes and busily admired each other. Even without the sequins and decorations, they all felt like special ballerinas.

"Now, we need to do some final adjustments, don't we?" said Hannah's mum, as she and Mrs Fisher set about making little tucks and seams on the bodices. They actually did the sewing while the girls were still wearing the costumes!

"Can we go and have a look in the mirror?" Meg asked when they had finished.

"Of course!" said Hannah's mum. The girls flew into the house to take a look in the Bakers' long hall mirror.

When they came back, the Glitter Girls showed their delight in their faces.

"Now, we need to sew on the decorations," said Mrs Giles, taking transparent boxes of shimmering sequins out of her work basket. "Are you ready to help us?"

"Go Glitter!"

The final preparations had begun!

★ ♥ ★ ♥ ★ ♥ ★

Hannah's mum made the headdresses and they looked fantastic. Now that the costumes were complete, the Glitter Girls wanted to wear them at every opportunity, but Hannah's mum pointed out that they needed to be kept in the best possible condition, so they were taken back to Mrs Giles's workroom for safe keeping until the competition.

The girls met up for rehearsals at every opportunity. With just a week to go, Flo finished the scenery. With the help of her dad and her sister Kim, she carried the two huge pieces over to Zoe's house, where the other Glitter Girls were waiting anxiously to see it. Flo had told them a little about it, but she hadn't wanted any of her friends to see the scenery until it was finished!

"Need any help?" Hannah asked, as Zoe opened the garage door so that the scenery pieces could be put inside. Fortunately, it wasn't raining but, even so, Flo and Kim had covered the scenery with lots of plastic bin bags so that it was protected.

"Can you take this bit, please?" Flo asked. "And I'll help Kim turn the end bit round."

Slowly and carefully, they rested the pieces against the garage wall.

"Come on! Let's see it!" Meg pleaded to Flo.

"Yes! Hurry!" Charly said excitedly.

"We've been waiting ages for this!" Hannah added.

"OK then, here goes," Flo said, revealing the scenery. ". . . So what do you think?"

"Hey, wow!" gasped Zoe.

"Flo, it's just great!" said Hannah and Meg.

"Oh, Flo!" Charly simply said.

The Glitter Girls had always known that Flo and her sister would do a great job. And now that they could see the scenery in its full glory, they were even more pleased with it. It had been painted with iridescent paints of icy blue, white and silver and it looked just like a snow-storm!

"Wait till you see it with light shining on it!" said Kim, switching on a torch that she had brought with her.

The scenery seemed to really come alive now – the snowy landscape shimmered in the light.

"Just imagine what it's going to look like with the proper stage lights!" exclaimed Charly. "Oh Flo, it's amazing! Thanks Kim!"

And the Glitter Girls started to hug each other in their excitement.

"Go Glitter!" they shouted; and even Kim joined in!

Chapter 8

There were only a few days to go before the talent competition! The Glitter Girls had rehearsed so much that they were exhausted. Charly had written and re-written her introduction to the ballet and Meg, Zoe, Hannah and Flo agreed that it was just the perfect way to introduce their version of the dance of the Sugar Plum Fairy to the audience at the Town Hall on Saturday afternoon. On Monday at breaktime, Charly, Meg, Flo, Hannah and Zoe were taking a well-earned rest in the playground.

"I can't wait until Saturday," said Charly.

"Me neither," agreed Meg.

"I'm kind of excited and absolutely terrified

at the same time!" exclaimed Flo.

Zoe laughed. "Yes, I know what you mean!"

"I'm totally scared!" Hannah confessed, kicking at the playground with the toe of her shoe.

"What do you mean?" Meg asked. "It's going to be great!"

"Yes, with the brilliant steps that you've choreographed for us," added Flo.

"And the great scenery and costumes!" said Charly.

"But we don't know what the rest of the competitors will be like, do we?" said Hannah.

As far as the Glitter Girls knew, there was only the one group of girls from school who had entered. They hadn't a clue who the other people in the competition were going to be.

"Well, there's nothing we can do about that, is there?" said Zoe.

"No!" agreed Meg. "Anyway, I thought we'd decided that we were just going to have a good time and enjoy ourselves!"

"Meg's right!" exclaimed Flo and Charly.

"Absolutely!" said Zoe, putting a comforting arm around her friend.

Hannah looked at the others and smiled. "I suppose you're right," she agreed.

"Go Glitter!"

They all jumped in the air in agreement.

★ ♥ ★ ♥ ★ ♥ ★

That afternoon, Charly's mum met the girls from school and took them into town to do some shopping on their way home. Mrs Fisher parked her car outside the Town Hall, right in front of the poster advertising the talent competition. Someone had stuck another piece of paper right across it.

"Hey, look at that!" said Flo, pointing it out to the others.

"What does it say?" Charly asked, poking her glasses back up her nose.

"Well. . ." Meg leant forwards to read the

sign. "It says 'Celebrity Judges Just Announced'!"

"What?" said Hannah, scrambling forward in her seat to read it as well. "Who?"

"It says they're Cindy Curtis – that's the woman from Media TV! – and . . . Tony Green!" shouted Meg.

"Tony Green?" exclaimed Flo, hardly able to believe her ears. "*The* Tony Green? From *Time's Up*?"

Time's Up was only the Glitter Girls' most favourite quiz programme on television!

"I think I am going to be sick!" said Hannah. She was just as excited as the others but she couldn't believe that two famous people were going to see the Glitter Girls dance in only a few days' time.

"Not in my car, you're not!" laughed Mrs Fisher. "Well, come on. Let's get out and get this shopping. Then we can get home for tea!"

The Glitter Girls bundled out of Charly's

mum's car and Meg helpfully unfolded Lily's buggy ready for her to climb into it.

"Isn't it great about Tony Green and Cindy Curtis?" Flo said. "I mean, we might get to meet them!"

She looked at the other girls – they were all grinning from ear to ear!

"Go Glitter!" they said.

★ ♥ ★ ♥ ★ ♥ ★

Because of all the other things that the Glitter Girls had to do, they weren't able to do much rehearsing on Tuesday. But on Wednesday afternoon, they were lucky enough to have some time with Mrs McArthur at the ballet studio for a dress rehearsal. She had agreed to see Charly, Hannah, Meg, Flo and Zoe to run through the dance of the Sugar Plum Fairy with their costumes on!

As soon as they arrived, the Glitter Girls climbed carefully into their costumes. Mrs Giles and Mrs Fisher did their hair and placed the headdresses on.

"Don't you look wonderful?" Mrs McArthur said, proud of her pupils. "Now, let's go into the studio. Mr Eng's got all the scenery organized already."

The Glitter Girls rushed into the studio behind Mrs McArthur.

"Wow!" said Meg, as the girls saw the scenery standing in place in the large studio. "I hadn't realized how much bigger than the garage this place would be."

"Me neither!" said Zoe and Flo.

"Well, I suppose that's why we're having a dress rehearsal," Charly pointed out.

"Yes," gulped Hannah, wondering if the Glitter Girls really were good enough to carry off their performance.

"Come on, girls," said Mrs McArthur, putting *The Nutcracker* CD into the CD player. "Let's dance!"

"Shall I do my introduction?" Charly asked.

"Yes, we want to see it exactly as it's going to be at the competition!" explained Mrs McArthur. "Places girls, please!"

Hannah, Meg, Flo and Zoe all took their places at the back of the stage while Charly went to the front.

"Look up, Charly," guided Mrs McArthur. "Don't forget to look right to the back of the auditorium as you speak loudly and clearly! But don't shout!"

Charly smiled and took her place with her arms held gently in first and her back leg bent, foot pointed neatly behind the front one as if she was about to *retire*.

"It was the night before Christmas. . ." she began.

★ ♥ ★ ♥ ★ ♥ ★

As the music drew to a close, Mrs McArthur, Mrs Fisher and Mrs Giles all burst into applause!

64

"That was splendid, girls!" Mrs McArthur said, going over to the Glitter Girls to congratulate them. "I am going to be so proud of you all on Saturday afternoon!"

"It was OK, wasn't it?" Hannah asked her friends.

"It certainly was!" agreed Meg and the others.

"I really enjoyed it!" said Charly.

"You were just brilliant!" Hannah said, holding Charly's hand. "I wish I could hug you all. But I can't because our tutus will get squashed!"

The Glitter Girls all dissolved into fits of giggles.

"Come on, girls," said Mrs Fisher. "I think we need to clear the studio for Mrs McArthur's first lesson!"

"And then, once we've got everything cleared away," said Mrs Giles. "I think you all deserve a special tea!"

"Go Glitter!" they all shouted.

Chapter 9

There were fewer than two days to go! The Glitter Girls met up after school and worked out who was going to be in charge of what and, with the help of Mrs Giles and Mrs Fisher, they started to make their final preparations after tea.

Ballet shoes were cleaned and ballet tights were perfectly folded and placed into the girls individual ballet bags. All of their costumes were looking fantastic under protective plastic covers. Mrs Giles had even sewn in special labels that she had got from the theatre where she worked. *Theatre Royal* they read. And then where it read *Artist* she had written the Glitter Girls' own names in their respective costumes.

Where it said *Character* Mrs Giles had written *Snowflake* or, in Hannah's case, *Sugar Plum Fairy*. The last line said *Production* and Mrs Giles had filled this in with *GG's Sugar Plum Fairy*!

The Glitter Girls' mums had agreed to help them into their costumes on the day and their dads were going to transport the scenery to the Town Hall and help to put it up when it was the Glitter Girls' turn to do their ballet.

"I've got to go and practise my cello," said Meg, looking at her watch when they were finished.

"Yes – I still haven't done my maths homework this week!" confessed Flo.

"Nor me!" said Hannah.

"I can hardly wait until Saturday, can you?" Charly asked.

"It's going to be such fun actually getting to perform it on a proper stage!" Hannah said, feeling the butterflies of excitement in her stomach already.

"Well – we'll have one last run-through to-morrow then!" said Zoe. "Then we'll be ready for the real thing!"

"Go Glitter!" they all cried as they set off home.

★ ♥ ★ ♥ ★ ♥ ★

It was Friday afternoon and all was going well with the Glitter Girls' final rehearsal when there was a loud thud and a piece of scenery crashed on to the garage floor.

Meg rushed over to stop the music.

"Uh-oh!" Zoe said, helping Flo to pick up the scenery.

"I'm really sorry, Flo!" Charly said, rushing to help her two friends. "I forgot that the scenery was there and I just carried on *pirouetting* back-wards. . ." Charly was really upset. "Look, I'm so sorry. . ."

"Well, I suppose that's what we need this last rehearsal for," said Hannah, looking anxiously at Flo, who was inspecting the scenery for damage.

The other Glitter Girls stood in silence, not knowing what to say.

"It's all right, isn't it?" Hannah finally asked.

"Ummm," Flo said no more and carried on her inspection.

After what seemed like absolutely ages, Flo finally turned to the others.

"Actually," said Flo with a very serious expression on her face. The Glitter Girls thought the worst. Oh no! The competition was tomorrow. . .

"Actually . . . I think it's going to be OK!"

Charly was so relieved that she rushed over and hugged her friend.

"You great big banana, Charly!" Flo giggled. And the other girls started laughing too. "You're meant to be dancing like a fairy, not like an elephant! Fancy crashing into the scenery like that!"

"I'm so sorry, Flo!" Charly apologized again. "Will it really be all right?"

"Kim may have to help me dab a bit more paint on it tomorrow," Flo said, "but I don't think any one will notice from the audience!"

"Come on then," said Hannah, looking at her watch. "Let's run through it once more from the top and then I think we need to rest until tomorrow."

So that's exactly what they did.

★ ♥ ★ ♥ ★ ♥ ★

At their homes that night, the Glitter Girls were so excited that they couldn't keep still. They all double-checked that they had everything ready on the lists that Meg had given them all. Then they re-checked it. Then they went through their own part in the ballet in their bedrooms. Finally, they tried to sleep. But it was really hard to do that when all they wanted to do was chat to their friends about tomorrow!

★　♥　★　♥　★　♥　★

"Are you girls all ready, then?" Zoe's dad asked.

It was late Saturday afternoon and the Glitter Girls had all met up at Zoe's house for a light tea. But they were all so excited about the competition that they couldn't eat!

"Come on!" Zoe's dad said. It was six o'clock and the competition was due to start at seven-thirty. The Glitter Girls wanted to be at the Town Hall in plenty of time to get themselves organized.

Charly, Meg, Hannah, Flo and Zoe were all standing in Zoe's garage checking they had everything. They were surrounded by things: each of the girls had her own pink ballet bag that held ballet shoes, tights and other bits and pieces. The scenery was being loaded into the back of a van that Meg's dad had borrowed. Hannah's mum had hung all the costumes in the back of her car.

71

"So," Meg looked around and was checking things off on a pink clipboard. "I think we've got everything."

"We're ready then," said Hannah, taking a gulp of air. It was almost time. Time to show everyone in town what they had been working on for the last month. Supposing something went wrong though? Or they made a mistake?

As if she could read her friend's thoughts, Charly put her arm around Hannah. "Come on. It'll be fine! We had our bad luck *last* night, when I crashed into the scenery!"

Hannah laughed. "I expect you're right!" she said. "Let's go!"

They all climbed into Mrs Giles's car. Hannah sat quietly at the back. *But supposing it does go wrong?* she thought.

★ ♥ ★ ♥ ★ ♥ ★

A whole procession of cars left from the Glitter Girls' homes to follow them to the Town Hall.

Brothers, sisters, mums, dads and grandparents – it seemed like everyone had turned up to wish the Glitter Girls well and to cheer them on! At last, they arrived at the Town Hall and, after finding some parking places, the Glitter Girls went with Zoe's mum to tell the organizers that they had arrived!

Chapter 10

The foyer of the Town Hall was packed. There were people of all ages registering their arrival with two girls who were sitting behind a big table. The Glitter Girls joined the back of the queue and, after what seemed like ages, they reached the front.

"Hi!" said one of the receptionists. "And you are?"

"The Glitter Girls!" they all said at once, making the two girls laugh.

"OK . . . I've got you here!" said the other receptionist, ticking the girls off on her list.

Then the first girl gave them a number and directed them to the dressing rooms. "It's curtain up at seven-thirty! Good luck!"

"Thanks!" said Meg, taking the number and leading the others in the direction of the dressing rooms.

"Hey look!" whispered Flo to her friends. "There are those girls from school!"

"Oh yes," said Hannah, feeling more nervous. They looked so cool about everything – there they were all leaning against the wall and chatting!

"Let's go over and say hello to them," suggested Charly.

"Oh no," said Hannah in a panicky voice. "I don't think we should!"

"Why not?" Flo asked. "They deserve as much luck as we do!"

"Come on!" Meg led the way.

"Oh, hi, you lot!" said the blonde girl they had spoken to in the lunch queue, smiling at them.

"Are you nervous?" asked one of her friends.

"Terrified!" Charly laughed.

Hannah just stood there, frozen to the spot and saying nothing.

Trying to make up for her friend's silence, Zoe said, "Can you believe how many people there are here?"

"It's amazing, isn't it?" the first girl agreed.

"Yes – I reckon they've all come to see Tony Green, don't you?" said a dark-haired girl in the troupe.

"I bet you're right! I can't wait to see him!" said Flo.

"Well, I think we should be getting off to sort out our space in the dressing rooms," Meg said, looking at Hannah, who had a very odd expression on her face. She still hadn't said anything.

"Yes, and us!" the other girls agreed.

"Good luck, you lot!" Charly and Flo said.

"Yes – break a leg!" Zoe laughed.

"And you!" the other girls giggled.

As they walked away, Meg took Hannah's arm. "What's up, Hannah?"

"Nothing. . ." Hannah was pale. "Except, I think I'm going to be sick!"

"Come with me then!" said Charly. "Let's get some fresh air!"

★　♥　★　♥　★　♥　★

After a few minutes, Hannah was feeling much better, and she and Charly headed back inside. She wasn't really going to be sick, she was just suffering from nerves. They found the rest of the girls in one of the dressing rooms.

"How are you, Hannah?" Meg asked, concerned about her friend.

"Feeling better?" Flo and Zoe asked.

"Much, thanks!" Hannah said. "I think it was just the anxiety about actually being here!"

"Come on, let's get ourselves organized then!" said Meg, and everyone laughed.

Now that they were actually getting ready, Hannah really did feel better. Something was going to happen at last, instead of all this waiting.

"What number are we?" Zoe asked.

"Number ten – out of nineteen," said Meg, who had, of course, got everything sorted. "We're to get changed and then we have to go to a special area at the back of the hall. That way we can watch the other performers until our number is called."

There was no more time for Hannah and her friends to think about being nervous. With the help of each other and their mums, the Glitter Girls got their costumes on and then each of them put on a special cape that Hannah's mum had borrowed from the theatre. The capes were going to protect their costumes while the girls had their make-up done. Each of the Glitter Girls' mums did her own daughter's make-up – they didn't wear much though. Just enough, Hannah's mum said, so that they didn't look all washed out on the stage under the bright lights. But they did all have a light brushing of glitter gel on their cheeks. Hannah's mum had bought it in Girl's Dream especially to make their faces shimmer like their costumes.

At last, complete with their headdresses, the Glitter Girls were ready in their costumes, shoes and make-up. After a final application of hair-spray, Dr Baker said, "Now let's take a look at you!"

"Don't you all look fantastic?" said Mrs Fisher.

"Don't forget, I'll be taking a video of you so that you can see yourselves later!" Mrs Eng reminded them.

"Do you mind if I take a photo of you as well?" asked Mrs Morgan, Meg's mum.

Mind? The Glitter Girls certainly didn't mind! They felt nervous, yes. But otherwise, they felt just great in their costumes and make-up.

The Glitter Girls found a space to stand together on one side of the busy dressing room. All around them, other people of all ages were getting ready for the competition.

"Are you ready. . . ? Smile!" Mrs Morgan said.

The Glitter Girls looked at each other, smiled and then said, "Go Glitter!"

The competition was about to begin!

★ ♥ ★ ♥ ★ ♥ ★

The hall was absolutely packed. But from where they were seated at the special place at the back, the Glitter Girls could see that their families had got seats right at the front.

"Good," Hannah whispered. "That means Flo's mum will have a good place to video us from."

Suddenly, the hall went quiet, and a woman walked up on the stage.

"It's the mayoress!" Charly said quietly, gripping Flo's arm.

"Good afternoon, everyone," said the mayoress. "I'd like to welcome you all to our talent competition. We've got nineteen acts to see and I know that all of them are very talented. Please enjoy your evening and join me in welcoming our judges who are seated in the balcony at the back." The lady pointed to the judges who stood up and waved at the audience and the competitors below.

The whole hall applauded!

The mayoress waved her hands in an attempt to quieten everyone down. When they eventually did, she said, "We're also delighted to have with us today Cindy Curtis from Media TV. . ."

The Glitter Girls grasped each other's hands. . .

". . .and Tony Green from *Time's Up!*"

The hall erupted with applause again!

"Now, everyone," said the mayoress when things were slightly quieter. "I'd like to welcome the first act on stage. Put your hands together for . . . act number one – *Groove It*."

There was more applause as the competition began.

81

★ ♥ ★ ♥ ★ ♥ ★

The Glitter Girls didn't have much time to think about being nervous as they watched the other acts. There was a magician, lots of different types of singers – from a folk singer, to a classical duet, to a boy band. There was also a boy who told lots of funny jokes, a man who did impersonations of famous people and even a puppet show! An elderly lady recited a poem that she had written, which the Glitter Girls thought was really good. Then a man went on stage to play tunes using a whole bunch of kitchen utensils as instruments. He managed to get a really good tune out of a rolling pin and a frying pan!

Suddenly, it was the moment they'd been waiting for.

"Could we have act ten on stage, please? The Glitter Girls!" the mayoress said.

"That's us!" said Meg, directing her friends towards the stage. "Good luck everyone!"

On stage, behind the curtains, the girls' dads had almost finished putting the scenery together. Meg's mum was crouched on the floor just below the front side of the stage, ready to start the music.

"Go Glitter!" she mouthed at the girls as they climbed the steps and took their places on the stage.

For once, the Glitter Girls couldn't reply.

Charly stood at the front of the stage, in position.

The curtain rose, and the Glitter Girls looked out into the sea of faces. . .

"It was the night before Christmas. . ." Charly said.

The Glitter Girls' Sugar Plum Fairy had begun!

★ ♥ ★ ♥ ★ ♥ ★

As the final chord indicated the end of their ballet, the Glitter Girls held their positions. Then the applause began! The girls could see Mrs McArthur standing at the back of the hall. She was clapping enthusiastically, her hands held high above her head. The Glitter Girls' parents were all cheering for them too. Even their brothers and sisters were waving approval.

In a blaze of happiness and exhilaration that the ballet was over and in the knowledge that they'd done their very best, the Glitter Girls made their *reverence* as the curtain dropped, and swiftly and quietly left the stage while their dads took the scenery away. Sitting back in their places at the back of the hall, the Glitter Girls looked at each other and hugged.

"Go Glitter!" they whispered happily.

★ ♥ ★ ♥ ★ ♥ ★

The rest of the show seemed to last for ever! The girls watched the remaining acts as patiently as they could. There were more singers, then a couple of musical acts, including a really brilliant teenage girl who played the piano from memory. Act nineteen was the girls from school, who did their routine to the latest hit from Geri Halliwell. It was really great and the Glitter Girls cheered their school friends when they had finished.

"They were good!" said Hannah.

Maybe they were too good and they would beat the Glitter Girls. . .

★ ♥ ★ ♥ ★ ♥ ★

As the modern troupe finished, the mayoress came back on stage and told everyone that the judges needed time to make their decisions.

"Please don't go away!" the mayoress said. "We only need fifteen minutes or so!"

The Glitter Girls were too anxious to go far. But before they could leave their seats, the other girls from school came over to them.

"We thought you were really good!" the blonde one said, smiling at them.

"Thanks!" said Meg. "You were pretty impressive yourselves!"

"Yes – cool music!" agreed Flo.

"Hey, look – my mum's over there," explained one of the other girls. "She wants to take a photo of us. See you later! Hope you do well!"

"You too!" Hannah said. She meant it. They'd been really good, so they deserved a prize.

★　♥　★　♥　★　♥　★

By the time the Glitter Girls had spoken to their families, the fifteen minutes had flown by and it seemed like only seconds later that the mayoress was calling everyone to take their seats because the judges had made their decisions.

Cindy Curtis came on the stage first, followed by Tony Green. After the applause had died down and the flashbulbs had stopped dazzling them (everyone had to take photos of their favourite celebrities!), Cindy and Tony took it in turns to speak about every act and how good each of them had been. Of the Glitter Girls, they said that they had liked the way that the choreography had reflected the music so well. They also made special mention of the costumes and scenery.

The Glitter Girls didn't know what to say, and just squeezed each others hands in happiness!

"Finally," said Tony, "we had to choose just one act as a winner from each of the junior and senior sections of the competition. It was so hard!"

"So, the winners of the junior section are as follows," continued Cindy. "The third prize in the junior section goes to . . . the Magnificent Marco! Marco, please come and receive your prize!"

Magnificent Marco was the magician. He raced on to the stage to loud applause to collect his prize.

When the hall had gone quiet again, Tony said "And the next prize goes to our dance act. . ."

The Glitter Girls froze in their seats! Had they come second?

". . .Act number nineteen – the *Go Girls!*"

The Glitter Girls clapped loudly for their school friends. But they were secretly disappointed – if one dance routine had come second, there was little hope that their ballet would come first.

"Finally," Cindy Curtis said, "we'd like to congratulate our winners in the junior section. . ."

The Glitter Girls couldn't bear to listen.

". . .Number ten – the *Glitter Girls!*"

The Glitter Girls had done it! They jumped up and down with sheer joy! They were so busy hugging each other that Cindy Curtis had to say, laughing, "Well, Glitter Girls! Would you like to join us on stage to collect your prize?"

Laughing and giggling with relief and delight, they rushed up on stage, applause ringing in their ears.

Both Tony and Cindy took their turns to congratulate the Glitter Girls.

"So, you're best friends too?" Cindy asked.

"We certainly are!" the girls all said at once, and then burst out laughing all over again.

"Well, keep up the hard work, girls, because you've got a bright future ahead of you," said Tony.

Then the winners of the senior section were announced, so by the time the competition ended it was really quite late. The Glitter Girls all agreed to meet up at Flo's house the following day so they could watch themselves on the video recording.

★ ♥ ★ ♥ ★ ♥ ★

When the Glitter Girls saw themselves on video the next day, they had to admit that they were pretty pleased with what they had achieved.

"Wasn't it great that the Kitchen Musician won the senior section?" Meg said.

"Yes – and the poetry lady and the singer both deserved their prizes, too!" agreed Charly.

"So, what are you going to do with your prize money?" Flo's sister Kim asked.

The Glitter Girls looked at each other. They hadn't even thought about that. They'd won a hundred pounds!

"I don't know," said Hannah.

"Perhaps we should split it and spend it in Girl's Dream?" Charly wondered.

"Or we could go to the cinema!" suggested Hannah.

"And we could have a pizza afterwards too!" said Zoe.

"They're all good ideas," said Flo, "but they aren't a very special way of using our prize, are they?"

"No. . ." the other girls had to agree with their friend.

"Of course, there is one really good way of

making sure that our prize will be used properly," said Meg.

"What's that?" asked Hannah.

"We could give the money to Pink and Fluffy!" Meg said, smiling.

Pink and Fluffy were the two donkeys that the Glitter Girls had helped to raise money for at the Donkey Sanctuary. They were very special donkeys, and the Glitter Girls loved them to bits.

Meg could tell by the happy expressions on her friends' faces that they all agreed with her.

"Go Glitter!" they all screamed at once!

Don't miss:

Party Poppers

"Hey, they look great!" said Zoe, helping herself to a sandwich from the plate on the Fishers' kitchen table.

"Yes – I'm starving!" agreed Hannah, tucking in as well.

"Thanks Mrs Fisher," said Meg, her mouth already full.

It was Thursday afternoon, and the Glitter Girls had come home from school with Charly's mum. Now they were in the kitchen having some tea.

"So, what are we going to do about this project?" Flo wondered aloud.

"What project is that?" asked Mrs Fisher, as she carefully cut the crusts from some of the sandwiches to give to Charly's younger sister Lily.

"Well," said Meg, starting to explain. "Miss Stanley has asked us to do some research about the town and the people who live here now and who lived here a long time ago."

"Miss Stanley divided the class up," said Flo. "And we've got to find out about life in the town in the twentieth century."

"Yes," explained Meg. "Other groups have to do the other centuries."

"Well, that sounds interesting," said Mrs Fisher.

"We've got four weeks to complete our project and we have to work as a group," said Hannah.

"I hope we can get everything done in four weeks," Meg said, being practical as usual.

"It sounds like ages!" Flo exclaimed.

"I know," agreed Zoe. "But Meg's right. I mean, we've got to go to the library and find out all the things that have happened here over the last hundred years before we can start writing or drawing anything."

"But I'm glad that we got the twentieth century, aren't you?" Hannah said.

"Yes," replied Flo. "We can get photographs and stuff, can't we? From that man in the market who has the bygones stall?"

"Good idea!" said Meg, grabbing a notebook from her school backpack and already starting to make one of her lists.

"And we can go and look in the church to find out the names of some of the big families who have lived here over the centuries," suggested Charly. "Then we could see if any of them are still living here!"

"Yeah, some of them must be still around!" agreed Hannah.

"I should think there are lots of people," Mrs Fisher said, sipping her mug of tea. "In fact, I think I know one of them."

"Who's that?" Meg asked.

"Mrs Greenfield's her name," Mrs Fisher said. "She lives in the home for the elderly that I visit every week. Lily really likes her, don't you darling?"

"Yes!" said Lily, her mouth now full of banana.

"Do you think she would talk to us?" Zoe wondered.

"I'm sure she would," Mrs Fisher confirmed. "She's always got time for a chat. I could ask her, if you like."

"Would you, Mrs Fisher?" Meg was sounding excited.

"I'll ask her tomorrow and let you know what she says," said Mrs Fisher.

"Go Glitter!" Meg and the others cried.